Sometimes
It Happens

Sometimes It Happens

Elinor Lander Horwitz

Pictures by
Susan Jeschke

Harper & Row, Publishers

Sometimes It Happens
Text copyright © 1981 by Elinor Lander Horwitz
Illustrations copyright © 1981 by Susan Jeschke
For information address
Harper & Row, Publishers, Inc., 10 East 53rd Street,
New York, N.Y. 10022. Published simultaneously in
Canada by Fitzhenry & Whiteside Limited, Toronto.
First Edition

Library of Congress Cataloging in Publication Data
Horwitz, Elinor Lander.
  Sometimes it happens.
  SUMMARY: A young boy discovers that sometimes
even ordinary deeds can make one a hero.
  [1. Heroes—Fiction] I. Jeschke, Susan.
II. Title.
PZ7.H7925So 1981   [E]   79-2687
ISBN 0-06-022596-3
ISBN 0-06-022597-1 (lib. bdg.)

This book is for
all the children:
Erica, Joshua, Anthony,
Angela, Reyna, and Eve.

Sometimes
It Happens

It was a hot night at the beginning of summer vacation. As Victor looked up at the tall black fire escapes and the fuzzy stars, he saw himself climbing a high ladder and stepping through the window of a burning building to rescue three frightened children. He brushed a bit of smoke from his eyes. He coughed quietly and then he smiled.

"The most important thing in life is to get a good education," Victor's father was saying to Victor and his sisters, Norma and Fran, and Ruthie from downstairs and Angelo from the third-floor apartment. "Just because school is out doesn't mean you can't improve your mind. Learn new vocabulary words, study maps, memorize the Gettysburg Address. I'm talking to you, too, Victor. You're not a baby anymore."

Victor looked toward the river and he pictured himself diving from the Brooklyn Bridge to rescue an old lady who had fallen into the water and didn't know how to swim. "Help, help," cried the old lady. "Don't worry. I'm coming. I'll save you," Victor called out.

"You don't know how lucky you kids are," Victor's father continued, sighing and opening his can of beer. "When I was a boy I had to leave school and go to work to help support my family. Maybe I would have liked to be a heart transplant surgeon or head of a big corporation or a college professor instead of being a plumber, but when you have no education you have no choices."

Victor looked out at the lights of the cars and buses crossing and crisscrossing in the street. He thought about being a cowboy way out west and galloping across the plains in the worst dust storm ever, to round up a herd of cows and buffaloes before they got lost.

"Maybe when Fran grows up she'll be a nurse," Victor's mother said. "Remember how she took such sweet care of you, Victor, when you were sick last summer?"

Fran shook her head. "When I grow up," she said, "I'm going to do something really different. I'll be an inventor or join the Marines or be a veterinarian and cure sick horses."

"Well, the veterinarian idea you should forget," said her mother. "You could get kicked in the head by a horse. When they're sick, they kick a lot."

"I know what I'm going to be," said Angelo, who was fourteen and getting a mustache. "I'm going to be a cabdriver like my dad, only I'll buy my own cab. When you own your cab you have a lot of independence. You get to be your own boss."

"I'm not staying in the city," Norma said. "I've

decided to be an archaeologist and travel all over discovering ancient cities and golden bowls."

"My goodness," said Mrs. Stansky, who had just walked over from across the street. "Your mother will miss you so far away from home. How about you, Ruthie?"

"Maybe a teacher?" Ruthie said in a shy voice. She looked at Victor's father and she could tell he liked her answer. But then she said, "What I'd really like best is to own a delicatessen and have all those good things to eat."

Everyone agreed that was a fine idea. They said they would shop at her store.

"Victor?" asked his father.

"I think Victor would make a great newspaper reporter," said Norma. "He really writes fast. About one word a minute and not on the line."

"Don't worry, Victor. I'll let you work in my delicatessen if you don't eat up all the pastrami," said Ruthie.

Victor looked at the cars and the taxis and the buses and the way their lights crossed and criss-crossed on the street. He looked again at the fuzzy

glow of the stars and the dark shine of the water. And then he said, "When I grow up, I'm going to be a hero."

"A hero!" said Fran, with a big spluttery laugh. "That's not a career!"

"You don't make the rent money being a hero," said Angelo.

"What do you mean when you say you want to be a hero, darling?" Victor's mother asked.

"Well," said Victor, "everyone knows what a hero does. A hero saves people's lives. He puts out fires and rescues babies. Things like that. Sometimes he gets a medal and has his picture in the newspaper."

Victor's father stood up and stretched. "Time for bed, children," he said. "Stick with your schoolwork, Victor, and when you grow up you can be an astronaut or a lawyer—or maybe even president of the United States. Lots of presidents didn't start out in homes that were any fancier or richer than ours. Abe Lincoln was born in a log cabin. In America any boy can become president."

"Or girl," said Norma.

"Yes—or girl," said Fran.

When Victor woke up the next morning he stayed
in bed awhile, looking out the window. He saw
himself rescuing wounded comrades while guns
went off all around him. He wiped his forehead,
imagining it was bloody. But he didn't pay any atten-
tion to his pain because heroes never do.

Then he heard the chirping of the two red birds
who were building a nest in the skinny tree that
grew in the alley. He went to the window to watch
them.

In the kitchen his mother and Mrs. Stansky were sitting at the table drinking coffee. Mrs. Stansky was talking about her new shoes which made her problem feet feel better. When Victor came in, she said, "I was glad to learn last night that you're going to be a hero, Victor. A hero is a handy person to have in the neighborhood. I hope you're here if I get hit by a speeding taxi one day when I'm walking across the street on my poor aching feet to see your mother. You could pick me up and carry me to the hospital faster than an ambulance."

Victor looked at Mrs. Stansky and he thought about picking her up. "Well," he said, "heroes have supernatural strength."

"Is that so?" asked Mrs. Stansky.

"Well, maybe not always," Victor said slowly, thinking hard, "but sometimes it happens."

After breakfast Victor drew a picture of a hero beating up ten men who had tried to grab a lady's pocketbook. He colored the hero's shirt silver with his best crayon.

Fran looked at the picture. "The hero has a pot-belly," she said.

"I think it's a very nice picture," said Victor's mother, and she taped it up over the sink.

"Boy, is that kid *spoiled*," Norma said to Fran.

Victor went outside to wait for his best friend, Joey, who was coming over to play ball.

When Joey arrived he was sweaty and out of breath. "I saw Ruthie over at the playground and she told me about your plans," he said. "I ran all the way. What's it going to be like when you're a hero? Will you rescue people right here in the neighborhood?"

"All over the city and in the country too," said Victor.

"The country is a really nice place," said Joey. "It's quiet and safe. There isn't any traffic."

"Yes," said Victor, "but there are dangers in the country too. Different kinds of dangers. There's plenty of work for a hero." He thought a minute.

"Here's the kind of thing that happens in the country," Victor went on. "A farmer's baby is playing in the barnyard and he gets afraid that the sick horse will kick him. You know, when a horse is sick it kicks a lot. So the baby crawls away from

13

the barnyard into the woods. And in the woods there's this wild snake. Just as the wild snake is about to bite the baby and poison it to death, a hero comes running down the path. He picks up the snake with his bare hands. Then he kills it with a karate chop."

"Does that ever really happen?" Joey asked. "I bet it's all a lie."

"Well," said Victor very slowly and thoughtfully. "Sometimes it happens." And as soon as he said this, one of the two red birds called out in its strange clear voice.

"Did that bird say my name?" Victor asked, startled.

Joey looked annoyed. "Of course not. He said 'tweet tweet.' That's what birds are *supposed* to say."

Norma and Fran came outside and began playing jacks.

Victor and Joey sat down on the bottom step. The weather had turned gray and windy and it looked as if it was going to rain.

"Our hero is dreaming of adventure," Norma

said to Fran. "Come on, Victor. Tell us what kind of rescue you're planning."

"So many things could happen," said Victor, and he looked at the way the wind was blowing the clothing of people crossing the street. "One day two old ladies are crossing the street in a terrible hurricane. They have problem feet and they have to walk slowly. Suddenly the wind gets under their umbrella and lifts them right up in the sky. The hero is inside eating lunch, but he has special birds in the alley who call his name when there's trouble. He hears the birds calling and he runs out to the street, where wires are falling down in the street electrocuting everybody, and he shoots an arrow up through the umbrella and very slowly the two old ladies come sailing down."

"Wow," said Norma, "that's pretty exciting. Do you really think such a thing could happen—*really?*"

"Well," said Victor, feeling very pleased, "*sometimes* it happens."

And as he spoke one of the birds sang out again and Victor looked toward the tree and at Joey and smiled.

"The birds are saying 'tweet tweet' and they're never going to say anything else because they don't know how. You sit on the steps and talk to your birds and make up hero stories. I'm going home for lunch," said Joey.

Victor looked more carefully at the two birds. One was bright red and the other more pink. He and Joey had noticed them just a few days ago flying back and forth with scraps for their nest. When he first saw them, Victor wanted to know what kind of birds they were. First he asked his mother.

"Most city birds are pigeons or sparrows," she said, looking at them through the window. "About these I just couldn't say. Ask Tony the Barber. He knows all about nature."

Victor ran down to the corner and asked Tony to come out and take a look at the birds.

"That's a very unusual sight," said Tony the Barber. "They must have come over from the park. Their exact name I forget, but I can tell you they're a special species. You call different kinds of birds 'species.'"

Victor stopped the social worker who was going to visit the Caseys. "I'm just a city girl," she said, putting on her glasses to see better. "Very pretty." She thought a minute. "All I can tell you for sure is that's no sparrow."

"I asked my brother the name of those birds," said Joey when he came back after lunch. "He said you call them Redbirds. There's Blackbirds and Bluebirds and Redbirds, and the Redbird almost never comes to the city."

"Well," said Victor, "sometimes it happens. Sometimes the special Redbird comes and makes his nest next to a special house where a special person lives and they get to be friends."

Joey snorted. "After I told my brother about the birds I told him about your plan to be a hero," he said. "You want to know something? My big brother thinks your idea of being a hero is dumb. So do I."

"Dumb?" Victor asked.

"Sure," said Joey. "It's all just make-believe—like the comics or television. My brother says you can't grow up to be anything you want. You've got to

have a steady job when you're grown up. You have to make a living. You want to starve? You want to be on welfare like the Caseys? You think you can live on medals? So what if you save the life of a billionaire and he gives you your own spaceship for a reward. Try and eat a spaceship!" Joey laughed.

"Well, what if you saved the life of the Queen of France and she gave you a mansion with roses growing all around, and what if the mansion had its own private amusement park and elephants and camels to ride and you could go there to live and take your whole family and all your friends? It would be a nice thing, wouldn't it?"

Joey shook his head and put his hands on his hips. "First of all, the queen lives in England and not in France, and second, a mansion doesn't come with elephants and camels and a private amusement park. It might come with a private golf course but you don't even know how to play golf!"

Victor sat down hard on the steps. "I have a stomachache," he said. "I'm going inside."

"Go ahead, hero," said Joey. "You think you're

so special and you have birds in your alley who say your name. Those birds are pretty dumb too. If they were smart they'd fly a couple of blocks away and find a really nice tree in the park."

Victor looked up at the skinny tree. The birds were gone. "My birds must be out looking for stuff to finish their nest," he said proudly. "They like my alley a lot better than the park. They get to have a tree all to themselves."

Joey looked angry again. "You know what I'm going to do? I'm going to knock down that nest and then they won't come back ever. Get this straight. Birds don't need people for friends. They have bird friends. When their nest gets knocked down they just go fly off someplace else."

Joey ran into the alley and grabbed a long stick. Victor ran after him. He stood by the tree with his arms stretched out. Joey ran around and around the tree trying to shake its skinny trunk. He poked with his stick toward the nest. Victor pressed himself against the tree, pushing at Joey and kicking at his legs. Joey grabbed him by one arm and tried to pull him away from the tree, but Victor suddenly

felt very strong. He gave Joey a big push that knocked him down.

Joey got up, picked up his stick, and then threw it away. "Oh, keep your old nest," he said. "Who cares about it? Anyhow, the dumb stick is too short. I'm going home."

Victor went upstairs. His mother was baking cookies to bring to a friend who was sick. Victor sat down and rested his head on his arms.

"What's the matter, darling?" his mother asked, coming over to sit next to him.

"Joey thinks my idea of being a hero is dumb," he said. "So does his brother. Joey says you can't eat a spaceship and heroes are make-believe and when you grow up you have to have a steady job."

Victor's mother put her arm around his shoulders. "You know, when I was your age I planned to be a movie star when I grew up. I thought about it all the time. I made up scenes—mostly love scenes and death scenes—and I practiced acting them out in front of the mirror. My mother and father wanted me to study shorthand and typing to become a secretary and so that's what I did."

"I never knew you wanted to be a movie star!" The idea made Victor laugh, but then he stopped and thought about it. "That's sad," he said.

"I don't know if it's sad," said his mother. "I had a lot of fun thinking about it, but I really liked being a secretary. In school I always felt nervous and blushed when I had to stand up and talk in class, so I probably would have been a terrible actress. But it was a nice dream, a special secret dream."

"Did you tell anyone about your dream?" Victor asked.

"No, never, until just now. I suppose I felt that would spoil it. But your dream isn't dumb, Victor. You really might grow up to be a hero if you remember that a hero isn't just someone who has big adventures all the time, like putting out fires and saving lives. Sometimes a person who's a secretary or a bus driver or a salesman or a college professor finds all sorts of chances to help people. If he's a real hero he doesn't wait around for something unusual to happen."

Victor thought about that. "You mean sometimes

it happens that an ordinary person who really isn't a full-time hero gets to help people in trouble?"

"Oh, yes," said his mother.

"He might even save some birds, or something like that. He might stop someone who was bigger than he was from knocking down the nest."

"That's exactly the sort of thing I mean," said his mother, smiling. "A hero cares about other people and their problems, and about birds and dogs and cats—and he doesn't just think of himself. He knows right away when there's something he can do to help."

Victor began to feel much better. "You mean if a hero lived in a building where someone new had just moved and that person had lots of troubles and no friends, this hero might invite him to his apartment and bring in pizzas and listen to his problems?"

"Exactly," said his mother. "Even if he really wanted to go to a party instead."

"And the next week that unhappy person in his building—the building has thirty-five floors—might get into an elevator," Victor said slowly, thinking

hard, "and inside there might be lots of fat people, and all of a sudden the elevator breaks and it begins to go down, down, down, and the hero races to the basement and he jumps into the shaft and with one mighty arm—a hero has supernatural strength, you know—he stops it just as it's about to hit bottom!"

Victor's mother laughed. "Well . . ." she said, and she gave him a hug. "Well . . ."

"Well," said Victor, pouring himself a glass of milk and taking one of his mother's best company cookies from the box she was fixing to bring her friend, because he knew she wouldn't mind, "I know that kind of thing doesn't happen often, but when there's a hero around, sometimes—sometimes it happens."

Elinor Lander Horwitz was born in New Haven, Connecticut, and received her B.A. from Smith College. She has written articles for many national magazines and has been a frequent contributor to *The Washington Star* and *The Washington Post*. She is the author of numerous books for children, teenagers, and adults. Her books for children include THE STRANGE STORY OF THE FROG WHO BECAME A PRINCE and WHEN THE SKY IS LIKE LACE.

She and her husband live in Chevy Chase, Maryland. They have three children.

Susan Jeschke, an accomplished artist and illustrator, has written several of her own books for children, including FIREROSE, THE DEVIL DID IT, and TAMAR THE TIGER. Born in Cleveland, Ohio, she now lives and works in New York City.